Fetish Warrior

By Princess Kink

Fetish Warrior
Copyright © 2021 Princess Kink

Table of Contents

Chapter 1: Multiple Orgasms 4

Chapter 2: Cursed Pussy 14

Chapter 3: Athena's Virgins 24

Chapter 4: G-Spot 33

Chapter 1: Multiple Orgasms

Lilla stretched and yawned, waking up from a much needed, deep sleep by a cozy fire. Her body was now completely healed from the frostbite thanks to the Greek warrior women and their ways of love. She looked around slightly confused. She could've sworn that she heard Halfdan calling her name, moments before he was swallowed by a black void.

"Everything okay?" asked Amara in her heavy Greek accent. Lilla nodded, stretching and flexing her fingers and toes.

"Yea...I think so. I just had the most peculiar dream..."

Amara walked over, her bare feet slapping loudly against the rocky floor of the stone hut. She sat down next to Lilla. Her white flaps that barely covered her ass and pussy folded in on themselves. They hung loosely from the tied rope belt around her feminine hips. Amara took off her dark leather armguards and massaged her forearms. "We have an oracle who might be able to help you, if this dream of yours is truly bothering you. Do you think it was more than just a dream? A message from the gods?"

Lilla wanted to pounce the Greek warrior and give her a big wet kiss. She was so beautiful, and her front flap was now completely to the side, exposing her slit. Amara caught her eyeing her vagina and lay on her back. She completely pushed the flap to the side and spread her legs for the nymph, allowing Lilla to get a good view of her spread pussy, tunneling all the way up towards the golden wetness of Mount Olympus itself.

Lilla pounced her, but not for a kiss. She instantly suctioned her lips around Amara's labia, shoving her tongue deep inside her salty, sweet birth canal. The warrior moaned like the Greek goddess of love, and firmly grabbed Lilla's purple hair. In seconds, she was dripping like a raging typhoon. Pussy juices dripped down Lilla's chin and created a trail of never-ending droplets all the way down her throat and between her breasts. Amara's drippings were clear and white. She was enjoying it too much and suddenly grabbed one of her armguards and bit into the hardened leather. Lilla could hear her muffled screams of ecstasy as her entire body began to shake and quiver violently.

Lilla's nose was touching Amara's overly sensitive clit, causing the Greek warrior queen to go into involuntary spasms. She wrestled the nymph and pinned Lilla to the ground, panting and sweating. Lilla spread her legs for Amara, and she dove into the nymph's hairless pussy, licking and sucking everything that stood in her tongue's way. Lilla climaxed almost immediately as she wrapped her legs and wedged her feet tightly around Amara's powerful upper body.

"That fast, eh?" said Amara, looking up from between Lilla's legs with a smile, the nymph's wetness still staining the warrior's lips.

"You never answered my question," said Lilla as Amara pulled herself up and lay down next to Lilla, running her fingers up and down the outlines of her perfect curves.

"What question?"

"What are Greek warriors doing in the Northland, particularly female warriors with barely any clothing or armor on…" Lilla was right. She'd seen no men so far at the Greek camp. Only fierce female warriors with gorgeous bodies that carried no signs of scarring or stories of previous encounters.

"We sailed here from the Mediterranean Sea with four large galleys. Everything was well until a storm split us apart once we reached the open ocean waters. We continued North, but storm after storm made it impossible for us to navigate… until we ended up in these frozen lands. We are warriors of Athena and through many prayers to the virgin war goddess, she granted us immunity and healing against Nature's shattering coldness."

"Virgin war goddess?" asked Lilla confused.

"Yes. We too are virgins in her honor," replied Amara, cuddling against Lilla.

—

"Wait…we just had sex…You mean to tell me that you still consider yourself a virgin even after all the passionate sex that we just submitted ourselves to?"

"No cock was involved," replied Amara immediately, as if she was used to being asked this question. "As long as we don't fill our pussies with any sort of erect manhood and dedicate our lives solely to Athena, she will continue to bestow her gifts upon us…this includes the reason why we can understand each other. Athena granted us the wisdom of languages. We can understand these Northmen here, as well as the nymphs of the forest, such as yourself…and you forest nymph, can understand our Greek language."

Lilla sat up, intrigued by this powerful foreign goddess and her many gifts. "And how do you ensure that she remains favorable towards you and your warriors? Do you have to bloody your swords?"

Amara looked at Lilla, slightly taken aback. "No. We don't bloody our swords unless we absolutely need to. We are not here as a raiding party."

Lilla shook her head and clicked her tongue. "I'd be wary if I were you. The warriors who visit our forest, the warriors of Odin…of Týr…of Thor…they please their gods by bloodying their weapons. They'll overpower you and take your virginity against your will, especially the way you're all dressed."

Amara huffed at the nymph, having taken offense at her comment. "It's a very seductive garment, is all I

—

meant by that!" sighed the nymph, still scared of these foreign warriors and their true intentions. At least with the Norse warriors and berserkers who visited her forest, she knew what their intentions were.

"Is that what they did to you?" asked Amara, looking Lilla straight in the eyes in order to detect any hints of a lie. "Did they take away your innocence against your will?"

"Well…not against my will. I seduced a powerful warrior, a berserker by the name of Halfdan. It's him whom I saw in my peculiar dream. I think he needs my help. I love him."

Amara exhaled sharply and then pulled herself up to her feet. She put on her leather armguards and then extended her hand towards Lilla. She pulled the nymph up to her feet and with a smack from her palm, shook the dust, earth, and sand particles which had clung to Lilla's perfect ass. She couldn't help herself and grabbed Lilla's bouncy ass cheek, spreading it to the side to reveal her tight, pink asshole. Amara wet her index finger on her tongue and gently pushed it through the barrier of her closed anus. She tapped against it gently, causing Lilla's asshole to slowly relax. She then pushed through, all the way to her second knuckle. It was warm and wet inside, and Amara could feel the nymph's heart beating through the thick veins in her ass.

"What are you doing?" asked Lilla, closing her eyes as Amara began to rub her clit with her free hand.

"Just relax," whispered Amara into Lilla's ear. The nymph had never experienced assplay like this before. Amara got down on her knees and replaced her index finger with her tongue. Lilla let out a moan from deep within her soul. Amara upped the speed of her clit rubbing as well and grabbed the nymph around her waist with her other arm. Lilla almost fell on her face as the sensations all came to a bubbling finale. She came loudly, thrusting her hips and asshole harder against Amara's tongue.

"Oh my gods!" squealed Lilla on all fours like a bitch in heat. Incredible wetness shot out of both of her cavities. She'd never squirted from her asshole before and was surprised by the sensation. Was that even possible, she thought to herself. Clear liquid dripped out of her asshole, joining the stream of pussy juices below, all the way down past her legs and knees, blending in with the dirt on the ground. "Wh-Where did you learn how to do that!" she panted with her eyes closed.

"We are a band of warrior women, who have only ever been with each other…of course we picked up a few tips and tricks along the way of virgin pleasures," replied Amara, licking the rest of Lilla's pussy and ass juices off her hands and chest. Some of the juices had squirted onto her big tits and the warrior queen freed them momentarily, making sure that she got every single drop of juicy goodness. "Come, let's put your mind to ease in regard to your berserker friend."

—

Amara led Lilla outside. The air instantly dropped to a nipple chilling temperature the moment the nymph dipped her bare toes into the snow. Even though it was freezing, especially for a naked body, the love that Amara had shown and given and slurped from Lilla had given the nymph the sustenance that she needed to thrive in this climate.

In the middle of the camp by an open field, an old woman was sitting next to a tall tree. She was muttering something to herself in a weird language. Her eyes suddenly rolled into the back of her head and she started to chant loudly, like an eagle's screech. "That's the oracle?" asked Lilla under her breath. The old woman replied before Amara had a chance to.

"I am many things Lilla, sex nymph of the Hardwood Forest. Some call me an oracle of Poseidon, but seeing as there is no ocean nearby that isn't completely frozen solid, I would settle for soothsayer witch." Lilla gulped and looked at Amara to see if the warrior queen approved of this. "Witch" wasn't a very endearing term and carried a negative connotation. Amara shrugged back and gestured for Lilla to step closer to the old woman.

"Hold out your hands," said the old woman. Lilla reluctantly stretched her arms out with her palms facing the sky. The old woman grabbed her hands like a praying mantis and ran her tough thumbs across Lilla's silky wrists. "Hmm…Beautiful…Gorgeous skin!

Pristine on the outside…yet, hurting on the inside. You've lost someone. Someone exciting. Someone who made you feel alive."

Lilla's hands trembled at the oracle's cold, dead touch. "That's right…I was separated from my friend, Half—"

"Halfdan" said the oracle before Lilla could finish uttering his name. "And he was more than a friend. A lover. A bear of a lover, I see…"

"What else do you see?" asked Lilla, intrigued by the old woman's ability to see right through her.

"I see darkness. Darkness has befallen your berserker, though not through death. No…that has already happened once. No…now he dwells within the warm confines of a womb with not even a light to accompany his trail."

Lilla tilted her head to side, confused by the oracle's nonsensical statement. "A womb? What do you mean?"

"I mean what I say…nothing more, nothing less," replied the old woman with her eyes closed. Lilla sighed and pulled her hands from her frigid grasp. The nymph looked sad. Somehow, this news about Halfdan caused her to worry even more about her grizzly warrior. "He's alive," enunciated the oracle, sensing Lilla's despair. She'd opened her cold grey eyes now and looked the nymph up and down. "Such a beautiful creature you are, filled with love…the love of nature."

"How can I find him?" asked Lilla, growing more and more uncomfortable by the oracle's lustful grin.

"The ground will tremble with each advance. It'll feel as though the world's scariest earthquake is right beneath your gorgeous little feet…"

Lilla took a few steps back. She was finished with this weird oracle who seemed to want her and obviously had a fetish or two of her own. Amara grabbed Lilla firmly by the arm and pulled her towards her perky tits. "Let's go," she whispered into Lilla's ear and took her back to the stone hut.

"What was she on about? What a peculiar woman!" hissed Lilla, pacing around the room.

"Yes, our oracle can be a little weird. I think she's getting interference here, between our gods and the gods of the North. It's making her go a little cuckoo. I'll help you look for Halfdan with the support of my warriors. But you must promise me something in return."

Lilla nodded intently. "Anything, you've been so kind to me."

"I need you to be happy and lock that happiness as an essence within your heart. I need your happiness to infect us and move through our ranks like Cupid's plague. We are all losing hope in this hostile land. Help us maintain happiness and a good heart through the aid of not just our gods, but your gods as well. Will you do that for us nymph?"

Lilla nodded with a big smile and stuffed her cold hands to be warmed through beneath Amara's flaps. The warrior moaned at the cold, icy touch of curious fingers climbing up and down her slit. They pounced each other to the ground again and went for yet another round of hot lesbian sex, as juices started to flow freely again, and eager tongues fed on the essence of survival.

Chapter 2: Cursed Pussy

Halfdan sheathed his sword for the fifth time inside the giantess' tunneling vagina. He'd thought about piercing her belly and cutting himself loose over and over again, but he always stopped himself from delivering that fatal blow. If Odin didn't want him to be here, then he wouldn't be. The Allfather had a plan for the berserker and the old warrior felt it burning in his loins. He was ready to shoot his blueballing load, but not yet. He wasn't deep enough. The giantess seemed to have grown, especially her birth canal. Halfdan made his way past many peculiar creatures, laying dormant in the dark and misty wetness. They were creatures, who like him, were trapped within the enveloping darkness of giantess pussy, forsaken inside the abyss.

"Hello?" said Halfdan, shaking his hand in front of the face of one of the demonic looking creatures. It turned out to be a she. She peered into the darkness as if she were waiting for something. She had extremely perky breasts with pointy dark nipples. Her skin was red and above her brow, two large horns protruded to either side. She had fangs for teeth and a serpent's tongue slithered from between those two needles. "What are you doing here?" asked Halfdan, unsheathing his sword for good measure.

—

"Quiet!" she hissed at him. "You'll draw his attention right to us!"

"Who?" asked the berserker, now unsheathing his seax and preparing his big, veiny muscles for battle. Something was wrong. All the demonic creatures around him were fixated on the darkened tunnel with their black eyes. A deep growl could be heard cutting through the hot air. The red and pink walls of the giantess' pussy shook with each approaching footstep. A large and heavy creature was approaching slowly, growling and hissing with each advance.

Halfdan stood very still and looked at the tunneling creature with six arms and two giant legs. The demonic creatures all whimpered and ran away. The naked, big-breasted female looked at Halfdan, surprised by the warrior's courage.

She tugged on his tattooed arm. "Follow me! Quick!"

Halfdan shrugged her off and tightened his grasp around his sword and dagger. "Odin!" he screamed in his deep voice. The behemoth making its way through the giantess' birth canal stopped in its tracks, taken aback by this hairy bear. Halfdan charged the towering entity of unholy power. It had twelve-pack abs and arms that could crush a mountain troll with ease. "If I should die, then let it be so!" growled the mighty berserker as he left a deep gash across the entity's right thigh. Before the creature could stomp him, he stabbed and twisted the seax deep into the monster's kneecap, severing cartilage and tendons. He then delivered another sharp cut from his sword, followed by a piercing stab. He repeated this combo over and over again, until the creature retreated back into the darkness, crying in pain.

Halfdan stood there, sweat dripping down his veiny arms and chest. The demonic woman with the horns along with her companions came out from their hiding spots. Halfdan noticed that they were all women. Their pointy breasts drove him crazy. He loved a good fuck right after some blood spurting carnage.

"H-How? How did you have the courage to take on that horrible creature?" she asked him, her tits moving side to side with each approaching step. She wasn't fully convinced that the berserker was on her side and kept a healthy distance between them, just in case he decided to turn on her and give her and her companions the same treatment he'd given the monster.

"Courage? There is no courage, only the Allfather. It's a matter of total faith and pure aggression!" he growled at her, forcing the demonic woman to increase the distance between them even more. The berserker wiped his blades on the edges of his headdress and sheathed them with a ring that echoed throughout the giantess' pussy. "Stay out of my way and we won't have a problem," he yelled at the demonic creatures multiplying by the dozens, all equally seductive.

"But…we'd like to repay you for saving us," said the woman, shaking her breasts and horns. Her red skin glistened with sweat and her tongue did little tumbles, performing for Halfdan like an erotic dancer. "Do you know what I can do with this tongue…what we can all do with our tongues?"

The berserker gulped and before he could refuse their services, the demonic woman had gotten on her knees before him and pulled out his cock with skillful and agile hands. Her tongue slithered in and out from underneath his foreskin. Halfdan groaned, having never felt such a thin and silky tongue before in his life. The slithering serpent's forked tongue slipped into his dickhole, licking deep inside Halfdan's cock. He inhaled sharply through clenched teeth. "What are you doing, woman!" screamed the berserker, not used to having his cock turned into a vagina of sorts.

"Just relax," replied the demonic woman. She licked deeper and deeper. Halfdan groaned loudly as his cock got ready to pump out the first rope of cum. His contractions pushed her tongue out and she cupped her lips around his ejaculating penis. She sucked and squeezed every last drop out, making sure not to waste a single sperm cell. She then pulled Halfdan carefully out of her mouth and turned around to her companions. She'd rationed the berserker's cum in her cheeks and spat it into the hungry mouths of the other demonic girls, carefully measuring the load squirt by squirt. She looked like a mama bird feeding her newly hatched younglings.

"What are you doing?" asked Halfdan, coming back to his senses.

"Do you have any idea, how long it's been since we've tasted the pure, creamy essence of man's seed?" said one of the demonic women right after gulping down her fill. "Far too long!" she screamed with laughter, answering her own question.

"She's right!" agreed another one behind her. All the women nodded and muttered their agreements in unison. Halfdan slowly unsheathed his sword again, which was all that was needed to instantly quiet everyone down.

"I don't care why you're so eager on ingesting cum, or what your purpose is here…but I have a quest which I need to fulfill before it is too late!" growled Halfdan, his pecs flexing and popping out like bulldozers.

"She asked you to give her a child, didn't she?" said the demonic woman who had sucked him off with the twirling of her adept tongue.

Halfdan looked over at her and pulled his headdress back a bit in order to get a better look at her eyes. "How do you know that?"

"Because, she asked us the same thing, many years ago. We were all men once…men from all over. Warriors, hunters, fishermen…you name it." The demonic woman suddenly smacked her lips and tasted intently with her tongue. "You've been touched by a Valkyrie, haven't you? I can taste it on your cum…the taste of borrowed time."

Halfdan was stuck on the part about all of them having been men once. "Wait, wait, wait…let's back up what you just said. You're all men?"

When the demonic women nodded in unison, Halfdan covered his mouth with his palm and burst into laughter. "Well, those are some mighty fine tits you have for being men. I'm gonna go now. It was nice talking to you."

"It's the curse of this place! The second the giantess pushed you through her lips into her pussy, a countdown started…only she didn't tell you about it. None of us knew either! You have three days to travel towards her ovaries and impregnate this giant bitch, or you too will start losing your humanity. Your testosterone will drain from you and all that will be left of you will be a pathetic little creature, like us! This place is pure estrogen and that's all you will have to live off of." The demonic woman who claimed to have been a Viking warrior many years ago, pointed Halfdan in the right direction with her feminine index finger. "Good luck, and may you reach Valhalla. None of us will…"

Halfdan saw the tears in her eyes and knew that she was telling the truth. He gave them all a salute of respect with his sword and disappeared quickly into the tunneling depths of the continuing darkness. He couldn't

---

move as fast as he wanted to. He was running on an incline and the ground as well as the walls were slippery with vaginal mucus. He knew that her ovaries would be deep and protected, and it would be a vertical climb to get access to them.

After a few more twists and turns upwards, Halfdan came across his next peculiarity. His eyes had gotten used to the blackness with a hint of dark red, the color of liver. In the corner, a tall warrior with a very similar complexion to Halfdan, grinded his two-handed axe loudly. Sparks flew high, lighting up his muscular and tattooed arms. He too wore a bear headdress. It was another berserker. "Step closer Halfdan, cursed by the Valkyries and the Allfather!" he said in the most familiar voice Halfdan had ever heard. It was his own voice…

"Who are you?" asked Halfdan, approaching the mysterious berserker cautiously with both his sword and seax drawn.

"I am you, had you not been stupid enough to get yourself cursed. I am an Einherjar, a different version of you, sent here from Odin's Great Hall. You interrupted my feast, lesser one…so let's make this quick."

Halfdan held his sword up and peered into the darkness. His counterpart was no longer flinging sparks up high and all was silent. Halfdan knew that he would need to perfectly dodge or block the first attack with both weapons. That axe had looked gnarly, a real powerhouse. "Ahh!" grunted the Einherjar, swinging his heavy axe through the air from his hip. Halfdan barely read the attack right in time for a successful parry. The axe head dug deep into the edge of his sword, causing it to slightly fold.

"Do you like it?" laughed the Einherjar, noticing Halfdan looking at his axe. "Dwarven craftsmanship…you cannot beat it. A gift from Odin himself for a lifetime of brutal war!" The axe was indeed beautifully crafted. The axe head was bearded and broad, with images of Týr and Fenrir etched into the steel. The thick wooden handle was wrapped in heavy leather straps, thick enough to block many a sword cut. Runes of all the gods lined the handle all the way down to the butt of the thick shaft.

Halfdan yelled as he flung the Einherjar's thick axe off his sword and swung hard for a riposte of his own. It was blocked and Halfdan was jerked back, almost losing his footing entirely. His nose felt numb and a warm wetness trickled onto his chest. The Einherjar had pummeled his nose with the butt of his axe, opening the lone berserker's nostrils like Mount Vesuvius.

"I am better, faster, and stronger than you Halfdan. I feast in the Halls of the Gods every day! Do you know what we do there? All the Einherjars attack each other and fight to the last man, every single day. The Valkyries then heal our wounds, and we drink ale to our heart's content. You could've had that…you could've been destined for that! You dumb motherfucker!" He came in for another heavy attack, which sent Halfdan flying across the dark, cave-like room. The old berserker got back up to his feet.

"Oh, give up! I'm more experienced than you! When was the last time you had an actual battle, that wasn't composed of shit for brains mountain trolls and permanently erect dwarves? You've grown rusty, old man. Out of touch, forgotten."

Halfdan grabbed the small leather pouch hanging from his hip. There was a small handful of shrooms left, dried little crumbs really. He popped them into his mouth then chewed and swallowed quickly.

"You think that will help you battle your better half? No drug will save you. You're already at Hel's gate, soon to be utterly forgotten!" cackled the Einherjar.

"You talk too much. If you want to fight, then let's fight!" snarled Halfdan, spitting blood onto the pink pussy floor below. The two halves of Halfdan attacked each other once again. Sparks flew high, illuminating the giantess' tunnel. The walls were squelching, as if her pussy was contracting with the onset of an orgasm. A faint moan, coming from outside the giantess' body, confirmed Halfdan's suspicions. She was probably fucking the mountain troll again. He had half a mind to turn back and castrate the troll mid fuck.

The shrooms hit him with added intensity, slowing down time and sharpening his senses. He parried the Einherjar's heavy overhead blow with his sword and stuck him between the ribs with his seax. The Einherjar said something to him, but the berserker was too far gone. Words didn't matter anymore. Only killing did…the thrill of victory was close at hand. Halfdan twisted the seax, splintering the Einherjar's ribs even more and stabbed him through the neck with his sword. He then grabbed the Einherjar's two-handed axe and decapitated Odin's warrior with his own dwarf-crafted weapon. The old berserker stood there panting, victorious once again.

Chapter 3: Athena's Virgins

Amara was able to rally quite a few volunteers to go searching for Lilla's lost berserker. She anointed them all with milk from her breasts, the milk of the mother. She claimed that the milk came directly from Athena's virgin tits and was what bestowed her everlasting gifts upon the warrior women, lost in the lands of barbarians.

"Why did you skip me?" asked Lilla, noticing that Amara had walked right past her during the ceremony. The sex nymph had looked forward to being sprayed in the face by Amara's sweet milk.

"Because you are not a warrior amongst our ranks. You cannot be. You have housed an erect cock inside the walls of your pussy. By definition, you are no longer a virgin and if we were to include you as part of our ranks as an anointed warrior, Athena's gifts would quickly turn sour and we would be left to fend for ourselves in this frozen wasteland." Amara could see the distraught look on the nymph's face and gently touched her cheeks with her hand. "Remember what I told you? Your happiness is what's most important. You are far more valuable than a mere warrior. You will be our beacon of hope and our guide through these foreign woods, which I bet you know like the back of your silky-smooth hands."

Amara caressed Lilla's neck and moved down to her perky breasts, pinching the nipples. "Come, I'll anoint you in a better way."

"We all will," chimed in another warrior standing up to her feet behind Amara. She slowly removed the thin white strap covering her huge, tanned breasts. They swung from side to side and were some of the most voluptuous tits that Lilla had ever come across. The rest of the dozen or so warriors all stood up together and followed suit. Beautiful Greek breasts were unleashed in a circle around Lilla, as the warrior women huddled together.

They each took turns licking and nibbling every part of the nymph's body. All ten fingers and toes were being sucked, licked, and sniffed simultaneously. Her legs, thighs, and pussy were being smothered. So were her arms, chest, tits, and belly. It was a symphony of tongues and fingers, going in and out of all of her holes. Her ass and asshole were being licked and fingered, then gently fisted. Lilla's mouth opened wide, like a fish gasping for air on dry land. She was out of her element but loved every single second of it.

Amara sat on Lilla's face, positioning her dripping wet pussy right over her gaping mouth. Lilla immediately licked and lapped up the Greek warrior queen's drippings, ingesting them as if they were the droplets of goddess' au jus. Everyone quite literally wet their palates, swallowing pussy juices, foot sweat, armpit sweat, hair sweat, even anal juices and mucus.

Amara suddenly looked back at the oracle. The old woman shook her head back at her and pointed into the distance with her crooked index finger. "You must leave before it's too late. I fear that the mighty berserker has met his match, within himself and borrowed time within the caverns of the timeless giant."

"A giant?" whispered Lilla, still trying to catch her breath from the five orgasms she'd just endured. She tried to stand up, but even that proved to be too much. Her clit was the most sensitive it'd ever been, and her pussy lips closing in around it like a taco only made matters even more unbearable.

"Rest for a second while we get our gear in order," said Amara with a chuckle. If there was one thing her and her warriors were experts in, it was war and pleasing pussy. Amara and the rest of her warriors gathered their swords and shields and sharpened their blades. They fell into ranks with Amara and Lilla in the front.

"Move out! Stay close and give those who would harm us no quarter!" yelled Amara, slightly turning Lilla on with her domineering ways. They crossed many hills, leaving cute little footprints in the snow behind them that would've fooled any enemy. Viking warriors would've for sure thought that they were a harem or a group of female slaves traveling by foot through the snow.

Though, the fact that their footprints were bare would've raised their suspicions, perhaps leading their thoughts to the trickery of Loki.

All was going well, until a small band of Norse warriors did pick up their trail. Two of Amara's warriors had lit the fire, allowing them to rest a bit before continuing through the cold. They had no idea where they were headed and solely trusted Lilla's intuition.

"Well, well, well…what have we here?" asked a young, blond warrior removing his helmet. He had the bluest eyes that any Greek had ever seen. Behind him, there were ten or so warriors all carrying round Viking shields. Some of the wealthier warriors had swords strapped to their backs. The less fortunate had axes dangling from their belts. They all grinned with a mouthful of perfect white teeth. They were all very well-groomed and tattooed from the top of their heads to their fingertips.

"We have no quarrel with you gentlemen," said Amara, stepping in front of her warriors, who'd all raised their shields and looked ready to attack at a second's notice.

"Neither do we," replied the young man. He then looked back at his companions and they all chuckled together. "We do however have needs that haven't been tended to in ages. You see, most women here complain about how cold it is. It's always too cold to fuck…but you lot, you don't seem to mind the cold one bit, do you? You walk around seductively with your tanned skin and peculiarly shaped swords and shields, with nothing but straps and flaps to cover yourselves. You're not from around here, are you?"

"Let me talk to them. I can satisfy all of their needs," whispered Lilla in Amara's ear.

"No!" yelled the warrior queen. "No, I won't have these puny little men ravage you over and over again. If it's a fight that you're looking for gentlemen, we are happy to oblige thee…"

The young Viking gulped and looked back at his companions, who looked back at him equally confused and wide-eyed. "Us? Puny?" he yelled, unsheathing his sword. "I don't want to kill you woman…"

"You couldn't kill me if all your gods were here to support you. Athena's might will erase you from this mortal plane, you puny little shit!"

The young Viking charged Amara. She deflected his sword cut with her shield and plunged her kopis directly into the meat of his thigh. The young man screamed in pain, tumbling onto the powdery snow, clutching his thigh with both hands. "I could've severed your artery and condemned you to death, warrior. In sparing you this fate, I hope that you and your warriors will think twice before attacking us again."

"Slaughter them all!" yelled the Viking warrior, still clutching his thigh. Amara beheaded him with a ringing cut and the rest of her warriors joined her side, interlocking shields. The Vikings attacked them, also locking their shields in a shield wall. Shields clattered loudly as Lilla could do nothing but watch the unnecessary turmoil. She decided to join in, swinging her purple hair at the Viking warriors like a whip.

Amara immediately turned around and pushed Lilla back with her shield. "No! Stay back, I cannot afford to lose you!"

"Why? Why am I so damn important all of a sudden!" screamed Lilla.

"Just do it! Stay back!"

The fighting continued. Lilla developed a tear in her eye, which instantly froze with the cold winter's wind. The first Greek warrior had fallen. Her beautiful curvy body fell to its knees, clutching the gaping gash across her belly. Her breasts had been freed and turned dark red as blood spattered onto them, dripping down towards her white flaps, staining them red as well. She looked at Lilla one last time, before life drained from her eyes.

The snow turned red and steamy. Heads rolled down the hills with twisted expressions and white, rolled back eyes. The Greek women stood victorious as they cheered, raising their bloody swords into the air. Only the one Greek warrior had fallen. The Vikings, having lost their inexperienced leader early on to Amara's wrath, had easily been dispersed and picked off. Lilla joined the panting and sweaty Greek women as they dug a grave for their fallen comrade. Her name had been

—

Maya and she was beautiful, even in death. Some of the warriors had cuts and bruises, and a few of them had had their straps and flaps slashed; rendering them completely naked. Lilla expanded her purple hair and touched each warrior with a few strands. She closed her eyes and healed their minor cuts and bruises.

The warriors walked up to her and thanked her with a kiss on the lips. The nymph, as requested, was quickly becoming their beacon of hope and happiness. They continued with their plans to make camp over the next hill. They also chose to wipe their footprints from the snow this time in case any more Northmen decided to come looking for them. "So, what are we looking for?" asked one of the warriors. They all looked to Lilla.

"Well, the oracle didn't give us much to work off of…Something about earthquakes and wombs and being lost in the darkness," said Lilla, looking down at her feet which had started to turn purple again from the cold. Without a single word, one of the Greek warriors walked over to her and grabbed her left foot. She pushed all of Lilla's toes into her mouth, making sure that her saliva got in between each freezing toe. Another warrior, who was missing both her breast strap and loin flaps, walked over and did the same to Lilla's right foot. The exhausted little sex nymph put her head back and moaned at the warm sensation of sweet spit and eager tongues. It was a win-win: they got to feed off of whatever sweat had frozen solid between her toes and she got to have her toes warmed up for her.

"Everyone stay here, I'm going to have a look around to try to get us some sort of bearings," said Amara, grabbing her sword and shield.

"Who is this berserker anyway?" asked another warrior, scooting over closer to the sex nymph with warmed through toes. The two warriors were still sucking on each foot like leeches, giving attention to her soles and ankles as well. Lilla didn't mind. She liked the sensation so much that she started touching her nipples with one hand, and with the other, she explored further down between her legs.

"His name is Halfdan. He's a battle-hardened bear with many kills under his belt. He has a long and thick cock with a beautiful cockhead." Lilla's mouth began to salivate just thinking about that Viking cock.

"What is it like getting fucked? You know…by a real cock," asked another warrior, seating herself very close to the nymph.

"Well, it's a fulfilling feeling. You feel the throbbing dick sliding in and out of wherever you choose to put it. It's inspiring. It's controlling and it's control at the same time. Whenever that cock throbs, you feel it inside you. It causes you to contract as well, gripping his manhood even better." Lilla was dripping onto the snow, sending steamy droplets of pussy juice straight to Hel.

She looked around and noticed that all the Greek warriors were fingering themselves. They wanted that cock. It was natural, no matter what Athena claimed. Lilla went down on the two warriors who'd sucked her toes first, causing them to orgasm almost instantly. She then moved on to the other warriors, servicing them one by one. She was no Viking cock, but she was close enough to soothe their senses after losing one of their own during a passionate battle.

Amara returned from her scouting trip, to see her warriors twisting and turning in the drippings of leftover pleasure. "I think I've solved the oracle's riddle," she panted, trying to catch her breath. She'd clearly ran back to camp as quickly as she could. Something had spooked her. Something tall and beautiful, shaking the earth with every gorgeous step.

Chapter 4: G-Spot

Defeating the Einherjar had taken its toll on Halfdan. Fighting something so closely associated with the Allfather had fast-tracked the Valkyrie's drippings which he'd consumed in the mountain troll's cave when he was on the brink of death. Halfdan was hungry again. Luckily for him, he was quite literally swimming in pussy juices. The old berserker licked the walls and noticed that the roof above him was swollen and a bit rougher than the rest of the skin lining this infinite tunnel.

He suddenly heard a loud moan and a gasp. Light blinded the berserker's eyes as something opened up behind him. He could hear something loudly tunneling towards him with incredible speed. It looked like the index and middle fingers of the giantess approaching him at the speed of light. Halfdan raised the great axe that he'd been rewarded through victory over the Einherjar and was ready to sever some fingers. One of the demonic women tackled him instead and pushed him out of harm's way. The giantess' fingers stopped and curled upwards towards the rough patch of skin, rubbing it profusely. Halfdan could hear the giantess moaning loudly on the verge of orgasm.

"What is—"

"Quiet!" hissed the demonic woman, her horns almost gouging Halfdan's eye out. "It's her G-Spot. You stimulated it by licking. You have to remember that everywhere you walk, touch, fondle, lick…she's going to feel it, especially if it's something as sensitive as her G-Spot!"

"I thought I was quite a bit deeper inside her vagina. Wouldn't the G-Spot be located way back there?" asked Halfdan, pointing towards the semi-blocked light coming from the direction plugged up by the giantess' long fingers. The light looked so enticing. He wondered if he could make a run for it.

"Don't…" said the demonic woman, grabbing the berserker's arm. "It won't lift your curse. You must fulfill your oath and impregnate her. It's the only way out of here. Giantess anatomy is different. Their G-Spots are located much deeper than what you're used to."

Halfdan brushed the demonic woman's hand off his arm. He was still not comfortable with her touching him, knowing that she'd once upon a time been a man…a Viking warrior, nonetheless.

"Still disgusted by me I see," she replied, shaking her head with disappointment. "I just saved your life and gave you knowledge about your curse…knowledge that we all would've loved to possess before it was too late! How about showing me some gratitude? I could've just let you wander around here aimlessly, cackling at you from the darkness until you lost your humanity and became an ill creature spawned from estrogen, like I am!"

Halfdan was surprised to see that she'd started to cry. She was completely female by all means. There were no lingering signs of a burly Viking warrior anywhere within her curvy, red body. "I'm sorry," said Halfdan, showing a kind of politeness that didn't come naturally to him.

"Just knowing that you were once a man…it made it difficult for me to wrap my head around that, especially seeing how skilled you are at wrapping your forked tongue around my cockhead…"

The demonic woman looked up at him with eyes bloodshot from crying. "Sometimes, I wonder if we'll ever get out of here. We've wasted enough time chatting about it. You only have one day left before you turn into one of us. Follow me. I know a quicker way into her ovaries." Halfdan decided to trust Fate's path. The Allfather knew what he was doing. This was all a test.

Halfdan followed her through a little slit to the side of the giantess' pussy walls. Slime covered it like ghostly teeth. He barely fit through it and the more he stretched it, the more the giantess moaned. He heard something like an ocean wave approaching him quickly. Before he could get out of the way, he was covered in sticky, clear mucus. The giantess was squirting all over his face and body, warming the berserker through as if he were on some sticky tropical island. He licked the free pussy juices, feeding his soul and body.

"Feeling better?" asked the demonic woman with a grin. She was turned on by the feasting warrior.

"I'm not eating you out," replied Halfdan, pulling the headdress well over his forehead.

"I never asked you to." They continued their journey up what turned out to be a mucus duct. Giantess vagina was vastly different when compared to human pussy. Instead of having two secreting glands near the opening of the vagina, giantesses had many mucus ducts deep within their tunneling and strenuous pussies. "Are you prepared?" asked the demonic woman.

"Prepared for what?"

"Prepared for your final test. The hardest test you'll face…even harder than defeating the Einherjar." The demonic woman pointed through the dark tunnel, which relaxed into a sexy shade of light red. The giantess' veins could be seen pumping blood quickly, running off of an excited heartbeat.

Halfdan held the two-handed axe firmly in his hands. His trusty sword and seax were sheathed by his sides as backup weapons. Though, judging by the confines of these ever-tightening walls, they may have served him better as his primary weapons. Halfdan looked up in awe at the stone statue standing idly in front of another narrow entrance. "That statue, it guards her left fallopian tube. No one's ever defeated it. Heimdall's

Watchman is what it's called. We haven't figured out how to defeat it. But if you can, you gain access to her eggs."

"How do you know what it's called?" asked the berserker without breaking his gaze from the glorious statue. It gave off an eerie vibe…cold and merciless.

"No time for that story…just attack it and if you're victorious, you'll break your curse," said the demonic woman in an extremely urgent tone. Halfdan's heart beat in his muscular chest. He charged the statue with all his might in the name of Odin, as he always did! The statue suddenly sprung to life, swiping and lunging at the berserker with jagged stone hands. Halfdan dodged his attacks and landed a hard hit square in his chest. The heavy axe rung a deep screech as the metal vibrated.

The statue grunted in an ethereal voice, sending shivers down the berserker's spine. He lunged at the bear warrior again, only to be met by a riposte that exposed a bright red light coming from the center of his chest. The stone fell to the squishy floor. The statue groaned clutching his chest. "Please…don't!" he pleaded with the mighty berserker. "You!" he snarled at the shadows behind Halfdan. Halfdan looked around and saw the demonic women, congregating like a pack of femme fatales. Their eyes glowed in the dark like vampire bats, causing the berserker to question his purpose.

"Please, don't kill me! I'm her last defense against those creatures. They're parasites that feed off of her

---

essence, weakening…corrupting her. She is not a bad woman. She is the fairest of all the giants. These vile little demons have spoiled her insides, and bent you, poor berserker, to do their will! You are their puppet!"

"He's lying!" screamed the demonic woman. "Halfdan, focus…you need to stay strong. Don't listen to his lies and strike him down! Hit the glowing red gem in his chest as hard as you can with your axe!"

Halfdan turned around over and over again, unsure what to do next. He then closed his eyes and thought of Odin and of Heimdall's great horn, Gjallarhorn. It suddenly became clear to him. He'd been deceived alright…He inhaled deeply. Once, twice, thrice. He started cackling like madman and began frothing at the mouth, letting the droplets of white, bubbling saliva run down his beard. He then focused his enraged gaze upon the demonic woman and charged her with such a passion, that the laws of physics stopped applying to him. He caught up to her in a matter of seconds, severing her deceiving head with one heavy swing of his axe. Next, he threw his axe at the second demonic woman he saw, trying to flee back up the mucus duct. He unsheathed his old friends: his sword and his seax and chased with glee, smirking through the whole blood spilling experience. He planted, sliced, stabbed, severed, pummeled, over and over again until they were all dead; every single one.

———

Halfdan panted within the mucus duct, looking at the results of his carnage. He barely remembered it. It came so naturally to him, a man of war and spillage. He turned around and walked towards the statue, still clutching its cracked stone chest. "They're dead. All of them," said Halfdan. He hadn't retrieved the axe. He didn't need it. He had everything he needed with him all along.

"You may pass," said the tall statue stepping aside. "And berserker, give her a child for Odin's sake!"

Halfdan nodded at the statue and journeyed through the long fallopian tube towards the nest of eggs. They were plump and well-rounded. Halfdan grabbed his Viking cock and stroked it thinking of Lilla. He came ropes worthy of Thor's perpetual fight against the giants, thundering his thick hammer. Halfdan's raging moan echoed throughout the chamber of her ovary. His thick, gloppy sperm almost sizzled onto the round eggs like a raw steak hitting a hot grill. The giantess' eggs turned and twisted, ensuring that every single sperm cell got its fair chance at the race towards conception.

Halfdan was suddenly swept off his feet. He was exfoliated out of the giantess' pussy as if he were a baby being born. The light blinded his eyes and the cold winter's soil of white crystals stung his skin. He looked up with blurry vision, his retinas still adjusting to the abundance of light. He didn't need his eyesight to be perfect. He knew exactly who was standing before him, rushing through the snow with gorgeous purple hair, blanketing life itself.

"Halfdan!" yelled Lilla in her fair fertile woman's tone. She hugged the berserker before he had a chance to pull himself up to his feet, knocking him onto his back with Lilla straddling him as if he were a stallion. The berserker was still hard from his recent ejaculation and his cock slipped inside her open walls, causing Lilla to let out a deafening moan that travelled across the field behind her. "Oh, how I've missed you!" she groaned as her eyes rolled back into her head.

Halfdan fought through the sensitivity of his still dripping tip. The sex nymph's vagina pulsed, squeezing out the remaining drops of leftover cum. There was a good chance that she'd get pregnant from the same cumshot which Halfdan had shared with the giantess moments ago before being uncomfortably expelled from her warmth. He held Lilla by her hips as her spine made serpentine movements, stimulating his cockhead from all directions. From behind her, a whole army of naked and semi-naked women ambled across the snow. They all held their swords and shields by their sides, ready to attack at a moment's notice.

"Get off me, we're under attack!" groaned Halfdan, his hands naturally travelling to the weapons hanging from his belt.

"Don't worry about them, they're with me," replied the nymph, her eyes still closed as she continued to ride

Halfdan's extremely sensitive dick. His abs were flexing and his pecs were hardening in all directions, causing him to writhe around as if he were in pain. Halfdan tried to push her off but Lilla had fortified her position with the help of her magical purple hair. "Don't stop, I'm cumming!" she squealed.

"Now!" screamed the old Greek oracle, who'd materialized from thin air. The decrepit woman stood next to Amara, who with painful eyes gave the order.

"Kill the Northman…cut out the nymph's heart while she's at her peak happiness!" The Greek warriors rushed across the snowy field in formation. Then, they spread out, encircling the berserker and still moaning nymph.

Halfdan's adrenaline proved to be enough to push Lilla off of him and he unsheathed his sword and seax. "Get up! They want to kill us both!" he growled without looking down at Lilla's sweaty body. She pulled herself up and together with Halfdan, they stood in the center, encircled by sexy warriors with swinging breasts hanging out and perfectly trimmed pussies up for display.

"Lay down your weapons, and we'll make your death a quick one, Northman!" said Amara in a cruel voice.

"Amara, what are you doing? I thought you were here to help me!" screamed Lilla, the look of betrayal burning in her gorgeous dark eyes. Amara looked back, slightly pained herself. She didn't really want to do this, but she had no choice. The oracle knew the worth of something as pure as a nymph's heart, especially one from a happy nymph. It would be enough of a sacrifice to offer them safe passage back home and out of this heathen land.

"I won't repeat myself again, Northman. Lay down your arms!" yelled Amara. Halfdan didn't reply, which was his signature death sentence. He didn't reply to those he was about to slaughter like cattle. "Very well…ladies! You know what to do." Amara's warriors started to close in on the berserker and nymph in unison. Halfdan swung his sword at the nearest warrior, slicing her shield in half with one powerful stroke. The warrior looked at her companions with a raised eyebrow. He truly was a bear, a bear who hadn't had time to put his cock away.

Halfdan's cock hung out, semi-erect and dripping into the snow. This was the first time any of the warrior women had ever seen a cock and it was distracting them to say the least. Even Amara's jaw hung open at the sight of it. They were all suddenly startled by the sound of the loudest moan they'd ever heard, rattling their ribcages. It was the giantess still lying on her back. Two warriors attacked Halfdan at the same time. He parried one but took a slice to the stomach from the second warrior. Blood dripped downward from his stomach, slowly painting his cock red.

———

They got ready to stab the berserker, in an attempt to deliver a fatal wound, but their attack was cut short by a trembling roar. It was the scarred bear that'd led Halfdan through the snowy mountains. Next to him stood the mountain troll, ready to defend his giantess queen. The bear and the mountain troll looked as though they'd patched up their relationship into something that resembled a friendship.

Amara and the rest of her warriors looked up in awe at the mountain troll's giant, hairy cock and balls, dangling and swinging in the cold winds with each mountainous step. On the other side of the field, something familiar popped its head up. They looked like little redheaded meerkats, spying on them over the snowy trenches and hills. Halfdan never thought in a million years that he would be happy to see Lord Redbeard and his dwarf warriors again. They charged over the hills, their erections glistening and throbbing. "You're all about to get fucked…literally," said Halfdan with a grin. The warriors tried to cover up their bodies with their small shields.

"No cocks can enter your pussies, right?" said Lilla, looking Amara in her terrified eyes. "Otherwise, you'll lose Athena's grace? Well, you're about to lose your virginity. Might as well lay down your arms and give up and I'll convince them not to take your innocence…the decision is up to you."

———

Amara considered this proposition for a moment. "I can't do that. What're you supposed to do against an army of horny little men? You're weak! You required us to save you from the cold, and yet you claim to be from this forest! You're a weakling Lilla. All I need is your heart and we will stand victorious over your berserker as well as these giants and little men! Athena will smite you all!"

At that moment, two ravens flew by and croaked loudly, circling them high above. Halfdan looked up and then at Amara. "I don't think that your goddess is here with you today. The Allfather watches me. He judges all, and who will die here today has been preordained long before you and I were ever born."

Amara let out a commanding scream and the warrior women locked shields with their swords protruding through the cracks like evil teeth. They all looked scared. They knew that they were outnumbered and the horniness quickly making itself towards them with short little bursting steps, sounded like centipede rape of throbbing will.

Halfdan slammed the shields with his sword, sending leather and wood flying everywhere. He stabbed the first warrior woman in the breast, causing her to wince and let out a high-pitched shriek. It felt wrong, slaughtering these gorgeous, tanned women of foreign origin. The bear joined Halfdan's side, clawing and biting and sending frothy saliva everywhere. A second warrior was swiped across her beautiful, plump buttocks, leaving behind a bloody bear claw mark.

"You think that I'm weak?" asked Lilla, finding Amara on the now scattered battlefield. The dwarves were almost there, sprinting as fast as their little legs could carry them. Before Amara could answer, Lilla wrapped her hair around her throat, squeezing the warrior queen until her face turned as purple as Lilla's hair. She let go right before the warrior queen was about to bite the snow.

Amara coughed and as she was coming back to her senses, she could hear the amplified moaning all around her. The dwarf cocks had found their targets and penetrated deep inside the Greek warriors' virgin pussies. Some of the warriors groaned at the stinging pain of their hymens breaking. Others had started to bleed, housing thick chodes for the first time in their warmth. "Stop! In the name of Athena, stop!" yelled Amara. It had no effect. It wasn't rape. The warriors had started to push back against the dwarves' thrusts. All parties involved were enjoying it. Amara looked around in horror, half jealous that she'd been forsaken and denied this pleasure, which deep down inside, she longed for.

Athena's blessings were lifted from her warriors and they instantly started to shiver. The dwarves took off their cloaks and wrapped their ladies' naked bodies in thick forest silk, like true gentlemen on a winter night's date, or fuck in this case. Amara was the only one left, naked and still protected by her goddess. The battle was over, and Lilla even healed the wounds of the two warriors who had been wounded. She turned around to heal Halfdan's wounds, but the berserker grabbed her hand before she could whisper the incantation under her breath. "I trust the gods and their decisions," he whispered to her, nibbling her earlobe.

Lilla hugged her man, stroking his thick white beard. Halfdan smiled and kissed her on the lips. "I'm sorry," said a woman's voice from behind him. It was the warrior who had delivered the cut to his stomach. Halfdan smiled at her and looked down at the wound, still pouring out small streams of blood.

"It was meant to be," he replied.

"This is ridiculous! Let me fix that wound. Maybe Odin wants me to fix the wound, and that's your destiny. Did you ever think about that?" snapped Lilla.

Before either Lilla or Halfdan could say or do anything else, the giantess crawled over and placed her large hand across the berserker's chest and stomach. In a second, Halfdan's wound was gone. Halfdan looked up at the giantess.

"Don't thank me, warrior. The Valkyrie told me to heal your wounds. She said that it wasn't your time yet and that you proved yourself more than what was needed…that you'd know who she was," boomed the gorgeous giantess. She then leaned in and said, "Thank

---

you Halfdan, for saving me from those demonic creatures and for giving me a child." She planted a gentle giantess' kiss right on his cheek and then took the mountain troll by the arm. Together they walked away, back to their love cave.

Halfdan grinned and looked at the beautiful snowy hills again. He took Lilla by the arm and clicked his tongue at the scarred bear. The three of them headed over the hills towards their next adventure, which destiny would unwittingly bestow upon them.

"Wait! What about me!" screamed Amara, the creepy old oracle by her side. She watched as her warriors walked arm in arm with their dwarf heroes, back to Lord Redbeard's keep. Athena's gift of languages had faded for everyone except Amara and the oracle. Though, the Greek warriors didn't need any gifts to understand their dwarf saviors. The language of love is universal after all.

"That's for you to find out," replied Lilla, whipping her purple hair into a long ponytail. She had her bears by her side and went off into the mountainous woods, in search of adventure and a new world; a world of life and death, and erotic fantasies.

9 798716 004825